Being a student of Mrs. Antle, she has inspired me both personally and scholastically. I'm sure this poem will inspire you just as it has me and my peers.

—Gabby Shapiro

In celebration of

_____

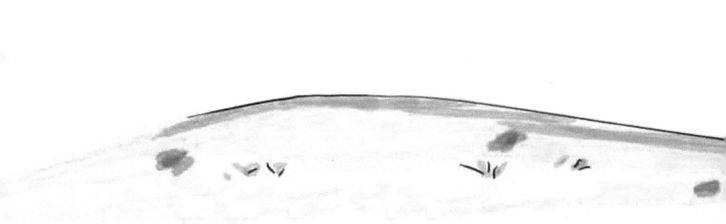

Given by

_____

ISBN 978-1-63630-390-1 (Paperback)
ISBN 978-1-63630-391-8 (Hardcover)
ISBN 978-1-63630-392-5 (Digital)

Cover and interior design by Elizabeth M. Hawkins
Illustrations by Justin Stier

Juvenile fiction/social issues/self-esteem/self-reliance

Covenant Books, Inc.
11661 Hwy 707
Murrells Inlet, SC 29576
www.covenantbooks.com

Someone
SPECIAL
by Peg Caryer Antle

DEDICATION

To Jeff and Chris.
"You are someone special, and I'm glad that you are you."

ACKNOWLEDGMENTS

Thank you to all of the children who have shared a part of their lives with me. My life is richer because of each one of you. A special thank you to Covenant Books for helping to make this dream a reality.

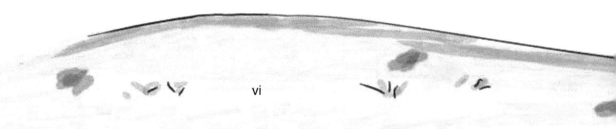

PREFACE

This book began as a poem written for my class of sixth graders as a means of encouragement and affirmation. Countless children have received it over the years. Before my retirement, my last class encouraged me to have it published so that you, too, could realize that you are special and worthy of celebration.

It is my hope that whether it has only been moments since your first breath of life or you are moments from your last, you will find yourself described on the pages that follow. It may be "your incredible good looks" or the promise that "you are a diamond in the rough," but rest assured, You are unique. There never has been and never will be another person just like *you*, and the world needs what you have to share.

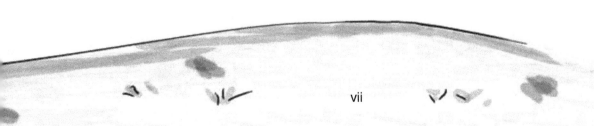

You are someone special,
And I'm glad that you are you.

It may be your eyes that twinkle
and show you're full of life
Or the gentle way you lend a hand
when others are in strife.

It may be your ability to solve a problem well
Or the gift you have to paint and draw;
you do them both just swell.

It may be your scientific mind that questions the unknown
Or the way you write the details of a story all your own.

It may be your faithfulness to do the
things others leave undone
Or your joyous laughter that fills the room with fun.

It may be your perseverance to dig a little deeper
when things get tough
Or the promise that you're a diamond in the rough.

You are someone special,
And I'm glad that you are you.

It may be your talent to work well with your hands
Or your dreams to visit distant lands.

7

It may be your insight into history
Or your detective style of solving a mystery.

It may be your melodic voice
Or the way you play the instrument of your choice.

It may be your athletic ability
Or your gymnastic flexibility.

It may be your love of books
Or your incredible good looks.

You are someone special,
And I'm glad that you are you.

It may be your flare for spelling
Or your knack for convincing your classmates
to do it your way by doing a great job of "selling."

It may be your sense of community pride
Or loyalty to remain at your best friend's side.

It may be that you are dependable
Or that you find knowledge indispensable.

You are unique, one of a kind;
Only you have your kind of mind.
I need what you have to share.
I want you to know I really do care.

You are
SOMEONE SPECIAL,
and I'm glad that you are you!

18

YOU ARE SPECIAL

Journal

When I was very young, before I even went to school...
I was told I was special because

_____

_____

_____

When I was in elementary school...
I was told I was special because

_____

_____

_____

When I was in middle school...
I felt special when

_____

_____

_____

When I was in high school...
my special gift or talent began to become evident because

_____

_____

_____

Now that I'm an adult...
I know that I am special because

_____

_____

ABOUT THE AUTHOR

In her long teaching career, Peg Antle taught five-year-old students to sixth graders. She believes that each of us has been given unique qualities and talents that need to be celebrated and shared. A native of Columbus, Ohio, Peg is the mother of two grown sons, grandmother of three grandsons and three granddaughters, and a great-grandmother of two great-grandsons and one great-granddaughter.

CPSIA information can be obtained
at www.ICGtesting.com
Printed in the USA
LVHW071145061121
702555LV00003B/16